Walt Disney's
Old Yeller

Senior Designer: Elaine Lopez
Editor: Sharon Fass Yates
Editorial Director: Pamela Pia

Walt Disney's Old Yeller copyright © 1953, 2001, 2005 Disney Enterprises, Inc.
Story adapted by Irwin Shapiro. Based on the book by Fred Gipson, published by Harper & Brothers.
Illustrations by Edwin Schmidt and E. Joseph Dreany.

$$\mathsf{C}\,\mathsf{E}$$

Copyright ©2008 Disney Enterprises, Inc. All Rights Reserved.
Published by Reader's Digest Children's Books,
Reader's Digest Road, Pleasantville, NY U.S.A. 10570-7000
and Reader's Digest Children's Publishing Limited,
The Ice House, 124-126 Walcot Street, Bath UK BA1 5BG
Reader's Digest Children's Books, the Pegasus logo,
and Reader's Digest are all registered trademarks of
The Reader's Digest Association, Inc. Manufactured in China.
1 3 5 7 9 10 8 6 4 2

Walt Disney's
Old Yeller

Illustrations by The Walt Disney Studios

Story adapted by Irwin Shapiro

Illustrations by Edwin Schmidt and E. Joseph Dreany

Reader's Digest
Children's Books™

Pleasantville, New York • Montréal, Québec • Bath, United Kingdom

$\mathcal{N}$obody knew where Old Yeller came from. He just turned up one day at the Coates's cabin, sniffing and snuffing and wagging his tail.

The Coates boys, Arliss and Travis, looked him over. Not that he was much to look at. He was big and clumsy and yellow in color.

He was full of tricks, too. Whenever anyone picked up a stick or a stone, he threw himself on the ground. He rolled around, howling and yowling worse than a wildcat. That was so you'd think somebody was beating him to a frazzle.

And he had to be watched. Old Yeller had to be watched, and he had to be told. If he wasn't, he'd steal a person blind.

Why, he could snatch a whole side of meat as slick as you please. Then, after he had eaten it all, he would look at you as if he didn't know a thing about it.

Old Yeller and Arliss took to each other right off.

"He's my dog now!" Arliss said. "He's mine! Isn't he, Mama?"

"I'm not sure we should keep him," Mrs. Coates said, and sighed. "If your Papa was here, he'd know what to do."

But Mr. Coates was miles away. He was driving their steers to Abilene, where he would sell them for cash money. And he would not be back for several months.

"Well," Mrs. Coates said. "Let Old Yeller stay for now. Then we'll see."

And whooping and hollering, Arliss ran for the pond, with Old Yeller following behind.

Standing still, Old Yeller looked as though he couldn't walk without falling over his own feet. But when he started running, he was like a streak of lightning greased with hot bear oil. He was swift and sure and a sight to see.

He was so fast, he once caught a good-sized catfish in the pond for Arliss.

Another time, he helped Travis drive some thieving raccoons out of the corn patch.

And he was a wonder at herding cows or hogs.

Then one day Arliss got himself into real trouble. He caught a bear cub by the leg. And he wouldn't let go, even when the big old mother-bear came charging at him, snarling and growling.

Suddenly, from no place in particular, Old Yeller came running up. He tore right into that old bear.

And while Old Yeller fought the bear, Mrs. Coates and Travis
pulled Arliss away from the cub.

Soon the big bear had enough of fighting and was running off through the brush.

After he saw that Arliss was safe, Old Yeller wagged his tail as if he would wag it right off.

"Oh, you crazy, wonderful old dog!" Mrs. Coates said.

"He's crazy as a bull bat," Travis said. "But he's a heap more dog that I had him figured for. I guess you'll let us keep him now, won't you, Mama?"

"You know I will," Mrs. Coates said.

But a few days later, a man came riding up to the cabin. His name was Sanderson, and he had lost a dog—a big yellow dog that was full of tricks. Old Yeller was his, and no mistake.

When Mr. Sanderson started to take Old Yeller away, Arliss screamed and carried on.

"You can't have my dog!" he shouted.

Mrs. Coates and Travis had to hold him back.

Mr. Sanderson looked at Arliss, then got down from his horse. "Just a minute, young fellow," he said. "What's that in your pocket?"

"A horned toad," Arliss said, and held it out.

"Finest horned toad I ever saw," Mr. Sanderson said. "You really want that old yeller dog? I'll swap you for the toad."

"Of course," Mr. Sanderson went on, "that toad isn't as big as the dog. Tell you what. I'm tired of my own cooking. You ask your Mama to throw in a good home-cooked meal, and the dog is yours."

Mrs. Coates smiled and nodded.

"All right. It's a swap," Mr. Sanderson said.

When dinner was ready, they all sat down at the table. Arliss and Travis couldn't help staring at Mr. Sanderson. Never had they seen anybody eat so much.

"Haven't had a feed like this in years," he said.

And so Mr. Sanderson got a horned toad and a home-cooked meal—and Arliss got Old Yeller.

"You're really my dog now, aren't you, boy?" Arliss said.

Old Yeller didn't say a word. He just wagged his tail and lay down in front of the fire. He knew he was here to stay.